CW00840155

HUGO
and the man who stole colours

First published in 1977 by Andersen Press
Limited

Picturemac edition published 1987 by
Macmillan Children's Books
A division of Macmillan Publishers Limited
London and Basingstoke
Associated companies throughout the
world

Cataloguing in Publication Data
Ross, Tony
    Hugo and the man who stole colours.
    I. Title
    823'.914[J]   PZ7

    ISBN 0-333-44546-5

Printed in Hong Kong

HUGO
and the man who stole colours

Tony Ross

MACMILLAN CHILDREN'S BOOKS

Hugo was bored. He had just finished the painting he had been doing all morning.
"It's a lovely day," said mother, as she prepared the lunch.
"Why don't you go fishing?"
So after lunch Hugo took his fishing rod and set off for the river.

The air buzzed with millions of insects. An old trout swam by as Hugo sat
gazing into the water.
Suddenly Hugo heard a faint sound.
He sat up, ears twitching. Yes, he was sure he could hear someone crying.

Hugo gently parted the rushes behind him.
"Anything wrong?" he asked the dark shape which sat huddled by the water.
The little figure turned around.
"*Yeeeech,*" shrieked Hugo. "A *witch!*"

"But I'm *not* a witch!" wailed the creature. "I'm a good fairy, and my name is Belinda."

"You *look* like a witch," said Hugo from a safe distance.

"Yesterday I changed myself into a witch for a fancy dress party," explained Belinda. " I used a spell from my beautifully coloured Book of Magic. But when I wanted to change back again, every single spell had vanished from the book and nothing was left but empty, white pages. Whatever shall I do? I don't want to look like this forever."

Hugo was stunned, but after a moment's thought he said, "Well, first of all, show me where you left your Book of Magic."

Belinda set off towards the wood, and Hugo followed. Soon they came to a pile of stones. Plunging her arm into a secret hiding-place, Belinda pulled out an ancient book, bound in dragon skin. "Look!" she cried, flicking the bare, white pages under Hugo's nose.

But something had just caught Hugo's eye.
One ghostly white toadstool stood out among a cluster of coloured ones.
Across the clearing more white toadstools led away into the trees.
"Someone is stealing colours," cried Hugo. "If we follow this trail of white toadstools, we might catch the thief."

"Here's another one," said Belinda, rushing off.
"And another," echoed Hugo.
The two friends followed the tell-tale toadstools all that afternoon and evening. At last, there were no more to be seen.
With failing spirits, Hugo and Belinda plodded on into the gathering night.
Finally, exhausted, they sank down on a grassy bank to sleep.

But in the morning they were in for a surprise.
Thump, thump, bang, bang!

Hugo pulled Belinda clear as a little door in the bank opened to reveal a white rabbit wearing crumpled pyjamas.
"You may as well come in for breakfast," he grumbled, disappearing down his hole again.
The two friends followed him into his cosy burrow.

Hugo and Belinda told the white rabbit about their search for the lost colours.

"Funny," growled the rabbit. "Yesterday afternoon I went to sleep in the sun, brown as usual, but when I woke up I was *white*!"

"We're still on the right track, then!" cried Hugo.

After breakfast Hugo and Belinda shouted their thanks to the startled rabbit and set off again on their search.
Suddenly, a large white animal jumped out at Hugo.
"A brown weasel turned white!" gasped Hugo, thinking he had found another clue.

The newcomer scowled.

"I am certainly *not* a weasel," he snapped. "I am an ermine, and ermines are always white."

Hugo blushed.

"A lot of ermines live in this neighbourhood," continued the superior animal, "and one of our favourite foods is common little pink larder mice just like you!"

Hearing this, Hugo rushed away. When he stopped to catch his breath, he heard Belinda calling from nearby.

"Hugo, come quickly," cried Belinda.

A trail of white bluebells led Hugo around a bend to an extraordinary sight.
Beyond, the familiar colours of the countryside stopped suddenly, giving
way to a cold, white landscape.

"The colour thief must certainly live here," said Belinda. "Come on!"

A terrible stillness lay over the strange land, but Hugo and Belinda walked on, and soon they came to a lone, white tower. "That must be the thief's house," whispered Hugo.
They carefully made their way towards the door, let themselves in and climbed the winding staircase into the darkness above.

At the very top of the stairs, they came to another door. Boldly they pushed
it open. Beside the window sat a curious little man. He was made *entirely of
colours*.
"I've been watching you through my telescope," he boomed. "What do you
want?"

"Sir," squeaked Hugo bravely. "We are searching for the coloured words from Belinda's book, the red and white spots from the toadstools, the blue from the bluebells in the forest and the brown from our friend, the rabbit. *You* haven't seen them by any chance, have you?"

The little man leaped from his chair, screeching with laughter. "Seen them? I've got them all here," he cackled, pointing at various boxes and jars. "I'm the man who steals colours! Why, only this morning I stole a beautiful brown from the trunk of a tree."

"We'll have our colours back, please," said Hugo.

"Oh, no, you won't," said the colour man, mumbling magic words that made him grow and grow until he reached the ceiling.

"You can't frighten us by *growing*," said Hugo firmly. "Anyone can do that."

"I bet you can't *shrink*, though," said Belinda.

"Easy," said the colour man.
Mumbling the magic words backwards, he grew smaller and smaller until he was tiny enough to ride a snail.
"I told you, I told ..." His words were cut short as Hugo sprang forward, tied his handkerchief around the man's mouth and bound his arms with a piece of string he had in his pocket.
Meanwhile, Belinda searched the room.

Soon she found a jar full of coloured letters. "These must be mine," said Belinda. Hugo grabbed the Book of Magic and dipped it into the jar. An angry gurgle sounded from the colour man as the pretty letters slipped back between the pages of the book.

"I'll see that you steal no more colours," said Belinda sternly.
She chanted a spell from her Book of Magic, and in a flash the colour man
was his old size again.
"Now all your power to make mischief has gone," Belinda continued as she
freed him. "But before I go I want you to take each box and jar of colours to
the window and tip them out into the countryside, where they belong."

As the colours spilled out over the ground, they all seemed to remember where they belonged.
Their work done, Hugo and Belinda set off for home. On the way Belinda murmured the spell to change her back into her old self.

In the woods they met their old friend, the rabbit. He was very happy to be brown again, but he couldn't quite believe that the funny little witch he had invited to breakfast that morning had turned into such a beautiful creature. "It's time I was going," said Hugo, and he set off across the stream.

While the rabbit sat puzzling over Belinda, Hugo skipped home trying to think up a tale his mother would believe.
What do *you* think he told her?